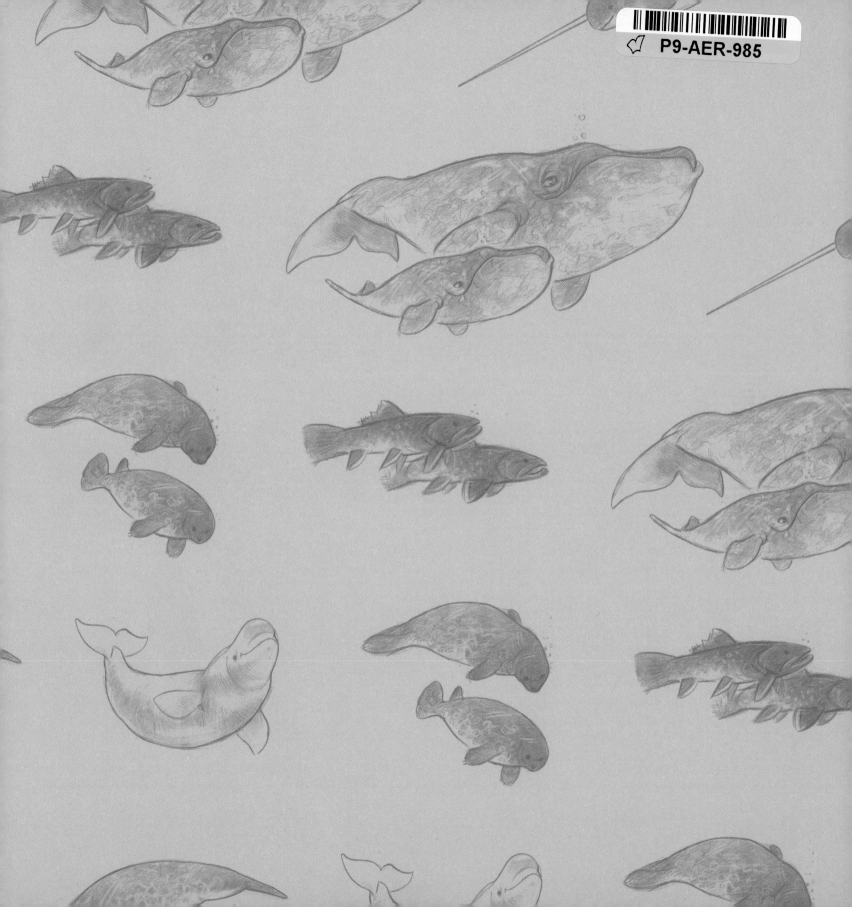

Ataatatsiakkanut. For my grandfathers.

Published by Inhabit Media Inc.

www.inhabitmedia.com

Inhabit Media Inc. (Iqaluit) P.O. Box 11125, Iqaluit, Nunavut, X0A 1H0
(Toronto) 191 Eglinton Avenue East, Suite 301, Toronto, Ontario, M4P 1K1

Editors: Neil Christopher and Kelly Ward
Art Director: Danny Christopher

This project was made possible in part by the Government of Canada.

We acknowledge the support of the Canada Council for the Arts for our publishing program.

Printed in Canada

Library and Archives Canada Cataloguing in Publication

Title: Grandfather Bowhead, tell me a story / by Aviaq Johnston ; illustrated by Tamara Campeau.
Names: Johnston, Aviaq, author. | Campeau, Tamara, illustrator.
Identifiers: Canadiana 20200344293 | ISBN 9781772272970 (hardcover)
Classification: LCC PS8619.O4848 G73 2021 | DDC jC813/.6—dc23

GRANDFATHER BOWHEAD,
TELL ME A STORY

by Aviaq Johnston

illustrated by Tamara Campeau

Grandfather Bowhead, tell me a story
of all the wonderful things you have seen.

Well, Little Arvaaq, in all my two hundred years
I've seen the northern lights running across the vast sky,
but they do not compare to the wonder of your very first breath.

3

Grandfather Bowhead, tell me a story of all the joyful animals you have met.

Little Arvaaq, I've met dancing seals who entertained us all, but they do not compare to the joy of watching you swim in the waves.

4

Grandfather Bowhead, tell me a story
of all the giants you have seen.

Little Arvaaq, I've seen icebergs the size of mountains
floating across the sea,
but they do not compare to the giant you are in my heart.

Grandfather Bowhead, tell me a story
of all the voyagers you have met.

Little Arvaaq, I've met geese who have travelled halfway across the world,
but they do not know the feeling of home that I have with you.

Grandfather Bowhead, tell me a story
of the most exciting thing you have ever done.

Little Arvaaq, I've swum through the fastest
currents you can imagine,
but they do not compare to the rush of
excitement I feel when we jump out of the
ocean to make big splashes together.

Grandfather Bowhead, tell me a story
of something amazing you have seen.

Little Arvaaq, I've seen walruses dive into the
very depths of the ocean to find clams to eat,
but that does not compare to the depth of my
love for you.

Grandfather Bowhead, tell me a story
of all the hard work you have done.

Little Arvaaq, I've broken through thick ice to help
our family breathe fresh air,
but all the hard work was worth it because it
brought you here.

Grandfather Bowhead, tell me a story
of all the friends you have made.

Little Arvaaq, I've befriended belugas and
narwhals and Arctic char,
but my friendship with you will last forever.

Grandfather Bowhead, tell me a story
of all the beautiful sounds you have heard.

Little Arvaaq, I've heard whales singing from far
across the ocean,
but no sound is more beautiful than the first
time I heard your voice.

Grandfather Bowhead, tell me a story
of the sweetest thing you have seen.

Well, Little Arvaaq, in all my two hundred years
I've seen everything you can imagine,
but nothing compares to the sweetness of
your sleeping breaths.

Inuktitut Pronunciation Guide

There are some sounds in Inuktitut that may be unfamiliar to English speakers. The pronunciations below convey those sounds in the following ways:

- A double vowel (e.g., aa, ee) lengthens the vowel sound.
- Capitalized letters denote the emphasis.

Arvaaq   ar-VAAQ   Bowhead calf that is still nursing.

Ataatatsiakkanut   A-taa-tat-SIAK-ka-nut   For my grandfathers.

For more Inuktitut pronunciation resources, visit inhabitmedia.com/inuitnipingit.

About Bowhead Whales

Bowhead whales are thought to be the longest-lived mammals on the planet. They can live two hundred years or longer. Hunters have even found ancient harpoon heads lodged in the blubber of these whales. Having the thickest blubber of any animal keeps them warm in the cold Arctic waters all year round. They have large heads and strong skulls, which they use to break through the thick ice in winter months. Bowhead whales like to be social. They like to slap their tails and flippers on the water's surface, and sometimes they even leap fully out of the water!

Aviaq Johnston is the author of the bestselling picture book *What's My Superpower?* For older children, teenagers, and grown-ups, she has written the award-winning novel *Those Who Run in the Sky* and its sequel, *Those Who Dwell Below*. She has also written the short stories "Tarnikuluk," winner of the 2014 Aboriginal Arts and Stories Award, and "The Haunted Blizzard," featured in *Taaqtumi: An Anthology of Arctic Horror Stories*. She grew up in Igloolik, Nunavut, and now lives in Iqaluit, Nunavut, with her dog, Sunny.

Tamara Campeau works digitally to create her painterly storytelling illustrations. Her work has a strong sense of lighting, naturalistic colours, and dynamic composition. She is strongly inspired by wildlife, children, and the environments they reside in. She uses this inspiration to add a layer of realism to her work. Campeau's illustration journey began at Dawson College, where she earned her associate degree in illustration and design. Shortly after, she furthered her studies at Sheridan College, where she obtained her bachelor's degree in illustration.

IQALUIT · TORONTO

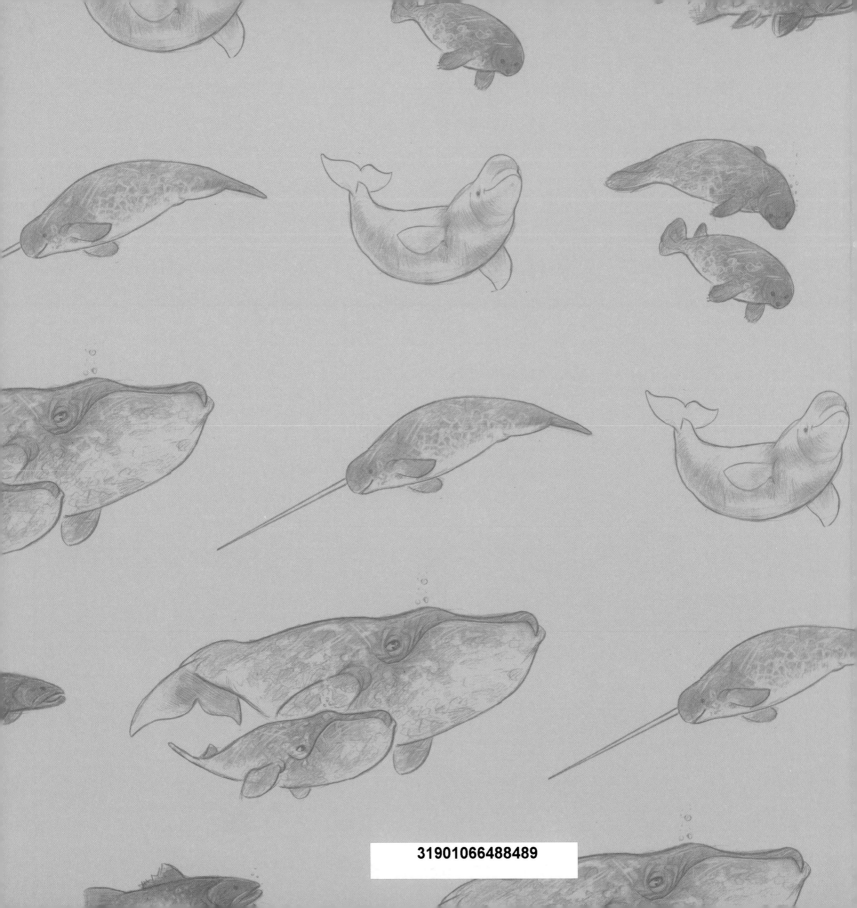